Steps To Christian Manhood; Or, Daily Words For Our Boys

Rosalind Marryat

Nabu Public Domain Reprints:

You are holding a reproduction of an original work published before 1923 that is in the public domain in the United States of America, and possibly other countries. You may freely copy and distribute this work as no entity (individual or corporate) has a copyright on the body of the work. This book may contain prior copyright references, and library stamps (as most of these works were scanned from library copies). These have been scanned and retained as part of the historical artifact.

This book may have occasional imperfections such as missing or blurred pages, poor pictures, errant marks, etc. that were either part of the original artifact, or were introduced by the scanning process. We believe this work is culturally important, and despite the imperfections, have elected to bring it back into print as part of our continuing commitment to the preservation of printed works worldwide. We appreciate your understanding of the imperfections in the preservation process, and hope you enjoy this valuable book.

Steps to Christian Manhood;

OR,

DAILY WORDS FOR OUR BOYS.

BY

ROSALIND MARRYAT,

AUTHOR OF
'WIVES AND MOTHERS; OR, READINGS FOR MOTHERS' MEETINGS.'

LONDON:
HATCHARDS, PICCADILLY.
1878.

LONDON:
PRINTED BY JOHN STRANGEWAYS,
Castle St. Leicester Sq.

CONTENTS.

First Week.

	PAGE
Sunday—What shall I do with my Life?	1
Monday—The Two Roads	5
Tuesday—True Manliness	9
Wednesday—Christ our Example	12
Thursday—What is your Ambition?	16
Friday—The Best Guide	19
Saturday—The Snares of the Devil	23

Second Week.

Sunday—Prayer	27
Monday—Work	31
Tuesday—The Cross of Christ	35
Wednesday—Purity	39
Thursday—Our Words	43
Friday—Temperance	47
Saturday—Honesty	52

Contents.

THIRD WEEK.

	PAGE
Sunday—CHURCH BELLS	56
Monday—COURAGE	60
Tuesday—TRUTH	64
Wednesday—THE POWER OF EXAMPLE	67
Thursday—FRIENDS	71
Friday—HONOUR	76
Saturday—STRENGTH	81

FOURTH WEEK.

Sunday—THE BREAD OF LIFE	85
Monday—GENTLENESS	90
Tuesday—THE FAVOURITE CORNER	95
Wednesday—GOD'S WITNESSES	99
Thursday—REVERENCE	103
Friday—GETTING ON	107
Saturday—HEAVEN OUR HOME	111

FIRST WEEK.

Sunday.

WHAT SHALL I DO WITH MY LIFE?

TEXT: 1 COR. XIII. 11.

'When I became a man, I put away childish things.'

TO-DAY is the beginning of a new week. To-day I want you to look life in the face, and see what can be made of it.

You are growing out of childhood into manhood. It is time for you 'to put away childish things.'

The difference between a child and a man is just this, that a child lives on from day to day, without any care for the future; a man has an aim in life.

A child is fanciful, changeable, easily turned aside by the opinion of others.

First Week—Sunday.

The first proof of a man is strength of purpose.

If you would act your part nobly in life, you must learn to be strong. Strong to resist evil, strong to seize all opportunities, strong to make the most of life; fearless in action, facing life with head erect, with stout heart and ready arm, working, watching—that is what God put you in the world for.

The danger that besets youth is carelessness, drifting to and fro with no real aim. You will never reach the goal in that way.

Above all things you must be in earnest.

To-day your life lies all before you; what will you do with it?

Remember, no man can live out his life twice over. If it is a failure, it is an unalterable one. If it is a success, it is an eternal one. You are a working man, but your life may still be a splendid one. St. Peter was only a poor fisherman. His life was spent in poverty, but he made it glorious by courage, by truth, by self-sacrifice, by love.

There is no reason why you should not live out as grand a life as any of God's highest saints. God's grace is still ready to help. To each of us the same command is given: 'Be ye therefore perfect.' It is only our laziness and love of self that stand in our way.

What shall I do with my Life?

Dare to be purer and nobler than your fellow-men: strive after it with heroic resolve and you will surely succeed.

If you turn away to-day and say, 'I can't,' you are taking the first step towards a miserable failure. You are spoiling your life.

And recollect also that no man can ruin his own life without helping to ruin other lives as well. By bad example, by mockery, by dishonesty, by sensuality, you are daily digging men's graves. You are murdering other souls as well as your own.

Your life is a great responsibility. God will ask you one day for an account of it. He is watching to see what use you make of it. His angels are watching you, men around you are watching. Play your part like a man.

'Quit you like men, be strong.'

PRAYER.

O Lord Jesus Christ, who hast come down from heaven to teach men how to live, give me grace to spend my life to Thy honour and glory. Make me earnest in doing Thy will, steadfast in aim, strong in purpose. Grant that being henceforth no more a child, 'tossed to and fro and carried about by every wind of doctrine,' I may grow up to true

First Week—Sunday.

Christian manhood, following Thee in all things, that so when Thou callest me to give an account of my life, I may appear before Thee without fear, and may be numbered among those who, being found faithful, shall receive the heavenly reward.

Hear me, O Lord, and help me for Thy love's sake. Amen.

Monday.

THE TWO ROADS.

Text: Ps. cxix. 30.

'I have chosen the way of truth.'

There is an old story of a hero who went forth into the world to win honour and a great name. And as he wandered, he came to a turning-point where two roads met. The one was smooth, all strewn with flowers, and fair faces beckoned him down it towards them. The other was rough and hilly, all overgrown with thorns; and a pale form, robed in black, called to him out of the shadowy darkness, bidding him turn and follow.

The hero hesitated long; but at last he said within himself, 'The upward road must needs be the best one: what matter that the way is dark and stony, if it leads me to the goal of honour?' So he turned away from the fair faces and the sunshine, to follow the voice which called him upwards.

And as he turned, the fair faces became ugly, mocking spectres, with twisting serpents hissing in their hair; the flowers grew wan and withered, and the sunshine was the fierce red light of flames. But in front of him, the path that had seemed so dreary was bathed in a flood of glory; and the pale form in black turned her face towards him, and her beauty was divine as she said, 'Thou hast chosen wisely: only virtue is happiness.'

You are not a hero, but you may be one; and so far you are like one, at least in this, that you stand now at the entrance of the same two roads. Manhood is the point where the two roads meet. Will you stamp your whole life for ever, by choosing wisely and well?

Two lives lie open before you. Will you be a man or a coward? Will you shirk what is hard and unpleasant, or will you face life nobly, conquering temptation and choosing death rather than the dishonour of sin?

Many voices will call you down the sunny, ignoble path: but remember they are the voices of mocking devils; though they speak fair, believe them not. The path is smooth, but 'the end of those things is death.' It is lighted not by God's torch of truth, but by the flaming fires of destruction.

You are young now; life is new and fresh to you: then believe One who knows and who tells you that goodness is the only thing worth living for. Only in goodness is true happiness. The only watchword worthy of a man is, 'Onwards and upwards.' 'Fight the good fight of faith; lay hold on eternal life.'

The age of heroes has not passed away. He is a hero who hating evil, wages war against his unruly passions, and by the grace of God strangles the serpents of sin which fasten themselves about his soul. Prove yourself a hero. Say from to-day with the grand prophet-king, the man after God's own heart, 'I have chosen the way of truth. Thy judgments have I laid before me.'

Prayer.

O Lord Jesus, who art our Guide on the road of goodness, show Thou me the way that I should walk in. Thou who hast created me for Thyself, make me a true man in courage, in faith, in purity. Shut Thou my ears to the devil's voices, that I may only listen to Thy call and follow Thee with my whole heart. Preserve me from the serpents of sin lest I be stung at last by the bitter remorse which follows wrong-doing.

Help me always to remember that sin is dishonour, that self-pleasing is cowardice; and do Thou, O most loving Jesus, who didst tread the road of pain and sorrow for love of me, teach me for Thy dear sake to despise pain and to conquer temptation, that, leading a holy and blameless life here, I may at last be presented pure and without spot before Thee. For Thy Name's sake. Amen.

HYMN.

The Son of God goes forth to war,
    A kingly crown to gain;
His blood-red banner streams afar:
    Who follows in His train?

A noble army, men and boys,
    The matron and the maid,
Around the Saviour's throne rejoice
    In robes of light arrayed.

They climbed the steep ascent of heaven
    Through peril, toil, and pain.
O God, to us may grace be given,
    To follow in their train.

Tuesday.

TRUE MANLINESS.

TEXT: 1 COR. XVI. 13.
'Quit you like men, be strong.'

'WHEN I'm a man I will do so-and-so,' we often hear from a boy's lips. Have you ever thought what it is to be a man? Have you quite made up your mind to be one?

Being full-grown will not make you a man. It means more than that. You must prove your right to the name, and win your title to manhood by manly deeds.

In olden days, however noble a knight might be, whatever his rank and position, his son could not inherit his title till he had first served his apprenticeship in courage, in truth, in loyalty. Then when he had distinguished himself in battle, or by brave deeds of any kind, and so proved himself worthy of the name, he was made a knight like his father, and silver spurs were given him as an outward sign of the honour he had won.

First Week—Tuesday.

Now-a-days there is no such apprenticeship in manhood required of a young man; yet remember, without courage, truth, and nobleness of heart, you have no claim to true manhood. A coward is not a man. A liar is not a man. He who lives a selfish, lazy, impure life is not a man, and never can be one, till he has changed his ways entirely.

Men may think lightly of what you do, and call you 'a good fellow,' all the same.

But you will not turn a bat into an eagle calling it one.

A bad shilling may pass for good coin for some time, but at last it will be rung on the counter and its worthlessness made patent. You may deceive others, and even think yourself, 'I am not such a bad one after all.' But when God rings you on His counter, there will be no mistaking your worthlessness.

Then quit you like a man. Be strong; 'Resist the devil and he will flee from you.' Shake off dull sloth and go out to fight God's battle in a world of sin by being the sworn champion of all that is good and holy.

It is told how the knights of old went forth to fight giants, to slay fierce dragons, to rescue oppressed innocence, to defend the weak. Your work to-day may be the same as theirs. There are the giants still of men's

True Manliness.

fierce ugly passions; there are the loathsome dragons of impurity, of drunkenness; innocence is still wronged by lies and slander, the weak are still oppressed by the selfishness and brutality of the strong.

You as a man will have plenty of noble work to do in your everyday life among your companions, in the field, in the factory, in the shop.

Will you begin to-day? 'Quit you like men; be strong.'

Prayer.

O Lord Almighty, who alone canst make men strong to do Thy will, rouse me out of my sloth and indifference. Thou who madest man in Thine own Image, teach me to form myself after Thy most holy likeness.

Make me courageous, truthful, pure, and strong. Arm me against evil and help me to endure hardness as a good soldier of Jesus Christ. Let me not fail nor be discouraged in my work for Thee.

Let not men's scorn or laughter move me from my purpose to fight for Thee even unto death. By Thy Cross and Passion, O Lord, make Thou me more than conqueror. For Jesus' sake. Amen.

Wednesday.

CHRIST OUR EXAMPLE.

TEXT: HEB. XII. 2.

'Looking unto Jesus.'

'FOLLOW me to-day, my children,' said a great king, as he led his soldiers into battle: 'my white-plumed helmet shall be your banner. I will lead you to victory.' On he dashed into the thick of the fight, and his soldiers bravely followed him. Amidst blinding smoke and roar of cannon, through the hail of bullets and the fierce onslaught of armed squadrons, they pressed forwards with eye fixed only on their leader, till the day was over, and the bloody battle was won for their king against his enemies.

You are a soldier too. Can you fight to-day as these men did?

They faced danger and death with heroic courage for an earthly king, because they loved him. Do you love your heavenly King Christ Jesus? Will you face your tempta-

Christ our Example.

tions to-day bravely, looking only unto Him, and conquering by keeping your eyes fixed on the example of the Captain of your salvation? He has led the way, and bids you follow Him. He has shown you how to fight against the devil, and to conquer. Will you obey that leadership?

It is morning now. Before nightfall you will have lost or won a battle for Him.

Will you be a coward and give in because Satan your enemy is strong, and you find it easier to run away than to fight: or will you be a worthy soldier in God's great army?

If you let an oath cross your lips to-day, you have allowed the enemy to conquer.

If you give way to angry or impure passions, you have betrayed your Captain.

If you are lazy in your work, dishonest in little things, untruthful, and selfish towards your comrades, you are losing the battle which your King bids you win for Him.

For the battle of our Lord God is against the devil and all wickedness: and when you do not stand up for the right, and speak out against what is wrong, you are nothing but a coward, running away because you dare not face a strong enemy and conquer for Jesus' sake.

Then think to-day, 'I am fighting for Christ Jesus, I am following Him;' and so get courage for your work. Let your motto be 'Looking unto Jesus,' and the thought of His help and presence will make you more than conqueror.

PRAYER.

O Lord Jesus, who art the great Captain of Thy faithful soldiers, give me grace to fight the good fight of faith manfully. Help me to follow Thee to-day with my whole heart, and let the banner of Thy cross lead me on to victory. Help me to win a battle for Thee to-day against wickedness and sin. Make me pure in heart, truthful, brave, and gentle. Teach me not to be afraid of being laughed at, but to stand up like a man for what is right. In my work and in my leisure teach me to remember Thy presence that I may never be led away to do what is wrong. And after I have fought and won Thy battles here on earth, give me a place in the heavenly home, and the crown of glory that fadeth not away. For Thy love's sake. Amen.

HYMN.

Soldier of Christ, arise,
  And put your armour on :
Strong in the strength which God supplies,
  Through His eternal Son.

Christ our Example.

Strong in the Lord of Hosts,
  And in His mighty power,
Who in the strength of Jesus trusts
  Is more than conqueror.

From strength to strength go on,
  Wrestle, and fight, and pray;
Tread all the powers of darkness down
  And win the well-fought day.

That having all things done,
  And all your conflicts past,
Ye may obtain through Christ alone
  A crown of joy at last.

Thursday.

WHAT IS YOUR AMBITION?

Text: Phil. iii. 14.

'I press towards the mark, for the prize of the high calling of God in Christ Jesus.'

Most men have an ambition of some kind. They have set their hearts on succeeding in some particular way. One man's ambition is to make a fortune. He toils year after year in a dingy counting-house, planning and scheming till his hair is grey and he can count his money by millions. Another man's ambition is to be learned. He pores over books all day and deep into the night, till he has mastered one science after another, and men come in crowds to listen to him and learn something of his great wisdom. A third wishes to achieve something which no one has ever done before. He would like to swim across the English Channel; to run a longer race than any one has yet done; to climb a higher mountain than any one has yet ascended. So he goes into training, exercises every muscle, lives on one diet, and after long perseverance he succeeds in this ambition also.

What is your ambition?

I want the text to be your answer. All other ambitions are poor and small by the side of that grand ambition after which St. Paul strove.

The Christian's ambition is a life of holiness. His aim, eternal life through Jesus Christ our Lord.

But do not think that you can win holiness without a struggle. It is hard to win money, hard to win fame, hard to succeed where many others have failed. Then do you think it will be easy to win Christ's prize?

The greater the glory, the harder it is to obtain it. The glory of saintliness is the highest glory of all. Then make up your mind to-day to set to work in earnest. 'Press towards the mark for the prize.' It is the only one worth winning, because it is the only one which endures for ever.

When you rise in the morning, say, 'I am a Christian. I have a great ambition; how can I get nearer to it to-day?'

Then kneel down and pray that God would make you worthy of the prize, and teach you so to live that you may succeed at last, so to run that you may obtain. You know His promise: 'Be thou faithful unto death and I will give thee a crown of life.

Prayer.

O Almighty God, who alone canst teach us to set our hearts on things above, fill me with a holy ambition to live a life of saintliness. Lord, I would follow Thee with my whole heart and be perfect as Thou art perfect. Make me noble and truthful to-day, patient and gentle, industrious and honest in my work, and a blessing to all those with whom I live. Create in me a clean heart, O God, and make me faithful unto death, that I may at last inherit eternal life through the merits of Jesus Christ our Lord. Amen.

Hymn.

Make us faithful,
Make us pure,
Keep us evermore Thine own.
Help Thy servants to endure,
Fit us for the promised crown.

Friday.

THE BEST GUIDE.

Text: Jer. iii. 4.

'Wilt thou not from this time cry unto me, My Father, Thou art the guide of my youth?'

You who are just going out into the world, answer me one question to-day. Whom have you taken as your guide through life?

Perhaps your secret thought has been, 'I need none to guide me. I can take care of myself. I am a man now, and can face the world alone.' How little you know of life if this has been your thought. Stop before it is too late, and consider what lies before you. This life is a long and dangerous journey for those who desire to find the heavenly home at the end of it. The wisest and best of us reach that goal travel-stained and weary—'through great tribulation.' Those who set out alone, never get there at all; for the narrow road of God is hard to keep, and self-will and carelessness lead many astray.

First Week—Friday.

Only He who is the Truth can show us the right path and hold up our goings therein that our feet may not stumble.

He who faces life without God, faces his own destruction. Many have shared your mistake—will you share their failure? Will you try in your own strength to conquer the world, the flesh, and the devil? Remember life is not mere child's play. Good wishes, good resolutions, will not take you to heaven. Every onward step must be bought by a struggle. Every victory over yourself won by the help of God. You cannot go forth to your work this day without meeting with temptations—temptations to drink, to bad company, to foul language, to slothfulness, to lies. Who, save God, can tell what snares the devil is setting even now for your feet? Will you face these unknown perils without a guide, without help?

Listen to God the Almighty Deliverer's voice, when He says, 'Wilt thou not from this time forth cry unto me, My Father, Thou art the guide of my youth?' Listen to 'your Father,' whose love will protect you. 'Your Father,' whose strength will help you to beat down the enemy under your feet. 'Your Father,' who will bring you safely into the land of promise.

And how can you take Him for a guide?

The Best Guide.

First, by prayer. Kneel down now and ask Him to be with you all through to-day. If temptation comes, lift up your heart with the prayer, 'Lord, help me,' and cry, 'In the name of God I will conquer.' So you will be able to crush down the rising temper, to shut your lips to the lie, to rouse yourself to honest, manly work.

Then rule your life and acts by what the Bible says. Do not trouble as to what is your mates' and comrades' way; but only as to what is God's way. Take a higher standard than those about you, and live fearlessly up to it. The Bible standard is the only true one, the only happy one. Vow, by the help of God, to live and die by it. Let your prayer be, Lord, 'guide me with Thy counsel, and afterward receive me to glory.'

Prayer.

O Almighty Lord, who didst safely lead Thy people of old, through the great and terrible wilderness to the promised land, be Thou my guide on the journey of life. Alone I dare not face the dangers round me. The devil is strong and I am weak. The road is long and dangerous, and I know not the way. Be Thou with me, and I shall fear nothing. Show Thou me the path of life that I may not wander, lost in sin and sorrow. Keep me by Thy side, strengthen me, uphold me, and beat down all mine enemies before my face, till I reach Thy home of peace to be with Thee for evermore. Hear my prayer, O loving Father, for Jesus' sake. Amen.

HYMN.

I know not the way I am going,
    But well do I know my guide;
And with childlike trust, I give my hand
    To the mighty Friend at my side.

The only thing I say to Him,
    As He takes it, is, Hold it fast,
Suffer me not to lose my way,
    But bring me home at the last.

Just as some helpless wanderer
    Alone in an unknown land,
Tells the guide his place of rest,
    And leaves all else in his hand.

'Tis home,—'tis home we wish to reach,
    He who guides us may choose our way;
Little we heed what path we take
    If nearer home each day.

Saturday.

THE SNARES OF THE DEVIL.

TEXT: PROV. v. 22.

'He shall be holden with cords of his sins.'

HAVE you ever watched a wasp caught in a spider's web? Have you noticed how slowly and relentlessly the single threads of that fragile net which seems so easily broken, cling round the imprisoned insect till it becomes the spider's prey? Surely you think the wasp is strong enough to break through the snare. But the spider lies hidden in a corner, and does not move till the wasp has exhausted itself by its efforts to escape. Then see, how, coming nearer, it flings first one thread round the wasp's wings, binding them to its side, then another and another, till the slowly winding threads have converted it into a helpless mass, and the spider can saw off wings and legs, and devour it at its leisure.

What you saw there is but the history of

many a man's soul taken captive by the devil's snares. It is one of God's parables in nature: its lesson is, Watch, lest the first slight threads of sin become the chain of misery and iron which binds you hand and foot, so that you be cast into outer darkness.

For a man's ruin does not come upon him at a single stroke. It is not by one sin that men mostly fall; but by a gradual yielding to temptation, an almost unseen falling off in holiness.

Our besetting sins are but single, fragile threads which are strong because they are so often repeated. We say, 'Only this once.' But one sin ever brings many. The bad habit grows so powerful that we cannot break away from it. The vice which a man loves, whether impurity, drunkenness, dishonesty, or unbelief, fastens on his soul, and the chains get stronger every day, till at last he is a helpless prisoner, led captive by the devil at his will. He has allowed his soul to be hampered by little yieldings, little cowardices, and so sin has got dominion over him. He would fly from evil now; but his wings of faith and prayer are powerless. He cannot pray and sin too. He is holden with the cords of his sins.

Then if you would not come to that terrible state in which a man cannot pray because he has lost all faith in God, cannot repent because he hugs his pleasant sins too tightly to let them go, beware of bad habits now. Resolve, by God's grace, to make a stand to-day against evil-doing. Draw a sharp line between right and wrong: and stand up boldly for righteousness and truth as in the sight of Christ your Lord. In the field or in the factory, in the shop or in service, let your motto be, 'I will behave myself wisely in a perfect way.' Make no excuses for transgression. Say not, 'It's but a white lie, after all;' or, 'A man must have his fling;' but rather with St. Paul, 'I keep under my body and bring it into subjection;' and with David, 'I hate every false way;' that so, 'being free from sin, and being made servants unto God, you may have your fruit unto holiness and the end everlasting life.'

Prayer.

O God, who seest my helplessness and foolishness, preserve me, I beseech Thee, from the devil's snares. Let me not be led away by little steps towards sin, but make me steadfast in resisting the first beginnings of evil. Set me free from the faults which ensnare me, and give me grace that I may run the way of Thy commandments with faithful heart. In my work and in my leisure, at home and abroad, teach me to live out a more perfect, courageous, manly life, to Thy honour and glory, who livest and reignest ever one God, world without end. Amen.

SECOND WEEK.

Sunday.

PRAYER.

TEXT: ST. LUKE, XVIII. 1.

'Men ought always to pray.'

WHAT is your answer to these words of Jesus Christ? Have you said, 'It doesn't matter about my prayers. Men haven't much time for such things. I've my work to see to?'

Or have you learnt to come to Christ simply as to your best friend, asking Him about everything you do—about your work and about your home, about your mates and about your master; about your temptations in the field and in the shop; about that extra glass of beer which you find so hard to refuse on Saturday night, and about the low, bad company which is so merry and enticing, but which leaves you a worse man for joining in it? Have you asked Christ to keep you from the oath which rises to your lips so easily, from the dirty thoughts which ought never to stain the mind of His servant, and from the white lies which get you out of scrapes?

My friend, if you have never come to Christ Jesus about these, and all other things which make up your every-day life, you do not know what prayer means, or why He says to you so earnestly, 'Men ought always to pray.'

'*Ought*,' because young fellows like you have to fight their way through a bad world where it is hard for them to keep their garments white.

'*Ought*,' because your passions are strong, and it is hard to say 'no' to yourself when the thing is wrong.

'*Ought*,' because without prayer the brute in you will get the upper hand, and you will grow coarse, and selfish, and lazy, with no care for God and goodness, no look-out beyond this life.

'*Ought*,' because if you come to Christ, and only if you come to Him, He will make a noble Christian man of you; teaching you how to do your work in the world bravely and well, for the sake of Him who died for you.

Then do not fancy any longer that your prayers do not matter. Kneel down now before you leave this room, and ask Christ to teach you every day more and more, what is the safety, the happiness, the strength, and the peace of the man who turns to God for everything, and who lives a life of prayer.

Prayer.

O Lord Jesus, who hast bid men 'always to pray,' teach me to come to Thee about everything. Be Thou my ever-present Friend and Helper, that I may know the happiness of a life of prayer, and flee to Thee in all my troubles and temptations. Let me not be daunted by the ridicule of men, or discouraged by the coldness of my own heart. Stir up in me the flame of earnest love and zeal, that praying more faithfully and heartily, I may obtain the petitions which I desire of Thee. Be with me on this holy day of rest, and let nothing keep me away from Thy house of prayer. Preserve me from wandering thoughts and lip-service, that I may not be among those who pray to Thee with their lips only while their hearts are far from Thee. Hear and answer these and all my prayers, according to Thy will, for Thy loving mercy's sake. Amen.

HYMN.

Restraining prayer, we cease to fight,
Prayer makes the Christian's armour bright;
And Satan trembles when he sees
The weakest saint upon his knees.

Monday.

WORK.

TEXT: JOHN, V. 17.

'My Father worketh hitherto, and I work.'

'I WISH I were a gentleman with nothing to do but to amuse myself,' the thought passed through your mind as you looked up yesterday from your field-work and saw a carriage roll past.

The desire is natural enough till you have learnt two great lessons of life: the one, what a splendid thing work is; the other, that no one in this world has any right to be aught else but a working man.

Do not mistake me; there are different kinds of work. A gentleman's work may not be quite the same kind as yours; but no man is worth a pin who does not seek out his work in the world, and do it bravely without flinching.

We were not set here to do nothing but amuse ourselves. God the Father works;

Christ our Lord is a worker; our highest privilege as God's servants is to be 'workers together with Him.' In that lies the whole secret of a noble life.

Then make up your mind to be proud of your trade, whatever it may be; as long as it is a useful, honest one, it is honourable. It is a grander thing to fill your position in life well, than to try to get out of it.

Good work is always beautiful, whether it be done in the field, the factory, or the shop. The man who dreads soiling his heart, is the true gentleman: not he who dreads soiling his hands. He is the worst snob of all who is ashamed of the place which God has chosen for him, for by filling that bravely and faithfully a man is alone made honourable.

Then how will you set about your work to-day? Will you make it mean and vulgar by lazy slovenliness; or will you work nobly as the 'servant of Christ doing the will of God from the heart?'

Will you do it cheerfully, feeling that you are working for your fellow-men, and so rejoicing in it; or as a poor miserable coward, who only thinks of himself and shirks what is unpleasant?

You know which is the grandest way of setting about it.

Up then, and do it.

Work.

Prayer.

O God, who hast given to every man his work, and hast commanded that none should be idle, make me to-day a true worker for Thee.

Keep me from lazy, unfaithful work: teach me to put my heart into it, that even in the smallest actions of my life I may glorify Thee. I thank Thee for giving me health and strength to earn my daily bread. Give me also, I beseech Thee, the spirit of wisdom and understanding, even as Thou gavest to Bezaleel, that whatever I set my hand unto, I may succeed and prosper therein.

Teach me to hate evil, even as Thou hatest it, that in the midst of temptation, I may, by Thy grace, keep clean hands and a pure heart, living in this world for God only, and for the life to come; that so when Thou shalt call me hence, I may hear Thy voice saying unto me, 'Well done, good and faithful servant; enter thou into the joy of thy Lord.'

Hear me, O Heavenly Father, and answer me for Jesus' sake. Amen.

Hymn.

Work is sweet, for God has blest
Honest work with quiet rest:
Rest below and rest above,
In the mansions of His Love;
When the work of life is done,
When the battle's fought and won.

Work ye then while yet 'tis day,
Work, ye Christians, while ye may;
Work for all that's great and good;
Working for your daily food,
Working while the golden hours,
Health, and strength, and youth are yours.

Working not your work for gold,
Nor for pelf that's bought and sold,
Not the work that pain imparts,
But the work of honest hearts;
Working till your spirits rest
With the spirits of the blest.

Tuesday.

THE CROSS OF CHRIST.

Text: Matt. x. 38.

'He that taketh not up his cross and followeth after me is not worthy of me.'

If you had ever been among German soldiers, you would perhaps have wondered why, here and there, one man among all his fellows wore, fastened to his breast, a little, plain black cross.

It seemed a thing of no value. It was made of iron only; it had neither gold nor silver, pearl nor jewel, in it; indeed it hardly showed out at all against the dark uniform. Why did he wear it?

If you asked him, you would see his eye flash with pride as he told you that it was the highest possible distinction that could be given to a soldier for courage in the battlefield. His emperor had granted it to him for some brave deed which had singled him out among the rest for the great reward.

His iron cross was the most precious thing that he possessed, and for nothing in this world would he part with it. True that such a cross meant facing pain and danger, but to the soldier it meant honour won. Who would not dare all to win the iron cross?

Would you also be a winner of it? Listen to Jesus Christ.

Such a cross He bore for our sakes. Such a cross He holds out to-day to you.

What is the iron cross of the followers of Jesus? Who are His cross-bearers?

For some of you it is the iron cross of poverty, of hard work done bravely day by day, of hunger borne patiently, of dreary homes, and pinching want. You may know who are Christ's cross-bearers by their faith and courage and patience.

For others the iron cross is the ridicule of their companions, the taunts and jeers of those who make a mock at a steady, sober, honest life. You may know His cross-bearers by their quiet, unflinching, steadfastness in doing what is right, and not caring for what the bad world says.

Christ's cross of honour is an iron one. Those who do not know its value, despise it.

They say, 'Shall we go through all this trouble; this want, this ridicule, this pain, only to be a cross-bearer? Let's take our own way, and throw off the cross of Jesus.' So the poverty makes them cowards, the want makes them dishonest, the hard work fills them with discontent. They have despised their cross of honour; they have branded their souls with shame.

We Christians say with joy and thankfulness, 'The cross is hard to win, but we will bear it. By earthly shame comes heavenly honour; by danger and trial we gain the reward of victory.'

Will you fight for the iron cross in to-day's battle? Christ holds it out to you, yea, He says, 'He that taketh not his cross and followeth after Me, is not worthy of Me.'

Prayer.

O Christ, the King of Glory, who leadest Thy soldiers on to battle against the world, the flesh, and the devil, be with me to-day as I go forth to my work. Make me one of Thine own cross-bearers, give unto me the iron cross of heavenly honour.

Teach me to be a true Christian hero in courage, in steadiness, in faithful fulfilment of my duty. Help me to brave the opinion of sinners, and to think only of Thy Word of command, that, fighting under Thy banner,

I may be ever true to Thee my Captain, and be among Thy victorious soldiers.

So when the battle of life is over, my soul shall rest in peace, and enjoy for ever in Heaven my Home the fruits of everlasting victory.

Lord, strengthen my weakness, arm me with the armour of righteousness on the right hand and on the left, hold up my goings in thy paths, that my footsteps may not slide, and keep me faithful even unto death. For Thy Love's sake. Amen.

Hymn.

Stand, soldier of the cross,
   Thy high allegiance claim,
And vow to hold the world but loss
   For Thy Redeemer's Name.

In God's whole armour strong,
   Front hell's embattled power;
The warfare may be sharp and long,
   The victory must be ours.

Oh, bright the conqueror's crown,
   The song of triumph sweet,
When faith casts every trophy down
   At our great Captain's feet.

𝔚𝔢𝔡𝔫𝔢𝔰𝔡𝔞𝔶.

PURITY.

Text: Matt. v. 8.

'Blessed are the pure in heart, for they shall see God.'

I HAVE read in an ancient book the tale of an enchanter who inhabited a wide, dreary forest, whither he lured men to their destruction.

Those who ventured into it lost themselves in the gloomy forest paths, and when, faint and weary, they longed for rest and refreshment, he appeared to them as a crowned king, at the head of a stately court of lords and ladies, offering them food and shelter if they would follow him.

He led them into a shining palace glittering with gold and silver, and placed before them an enchanted cup, out of which he bade them drink.

As they raised it to their lips, they became cold and stiff as marble, so that they could no longer turn and flee.

Their eyes were opened, and they saw

the enchanter, not now as a king, but as a hideous monster, surrounded by a rabble crowd of human forms all with the heads of beasts. One had the face of a wolf with fiery eyes and open jaws; another resembled a hissing serpent; a third was like a squatting toad. And if the man had drunk deeply of that cup, he himself became like the loathsome forms which surrounded the enchanter. Dumb and unable to warn his fellow-men of their fate, he was forced to join the hideous crew and lead other wanderers to a like destruction.

Does anything like this ever happen in real life, think you?

There is a dark wood, called the wood of error, into which men wander recklessly in youth. They want to 'see life'—and the enchanter comes,—Satan promising them happiness. Sin seems very pleasant, and a man, they think, must have his fling.

So they drink of the poisoned cup and the devil is made glad.

Who can wreck another's soul and leave his own uninjured? Who can defile God's temple in the heart and not be thereby defiled?

It is thus men lose the self-respect which is their bulwark against moral evil. They blunt the noble impulses which raise them

Purity.

above the brutes. They blur their divinity, and stamp their souls with the sensual animal type.

Not Godwards they look—but earthwards. They have forsaken the white-robed company of the Christ, to follow the rabble crew of the enchanter. Alas for them, even if they break loose from that base society, can life ever again be quite what it might have been had they guarded as their choicest treasure, the blessing granted to man and woman alike, of the pure in heart?

Are you on the borders of that dark wood of error?

Is the enchanter holding out that fatal cup for the first time to-day?

'Pray that ye enter not into temptation.'

Prayer.

O God, whose blessed Son was manifested that He might destroy the works of the devil, and make us sons of God and heirs of eternal life, grant to us that having this hope we may purify ourselves even as He is pure, that when He shall appear again with power and great glory, we may be made like unto Him in His eternal and glorious kingdom; where, with Thee, O Father, and Thee the Holy Ghost, He liveth and reigneth ever one God, world without end. Amen.

Hymn.

Blest are the pure in heart,
  For they shall see their God;
The secret of the Lord is theirs,
  Their soul is Christ's abode.

The Lord that left the heavens,
  Our life and peace to bring,
To dwell in lowliness with men,
  Their pattern and their King.

He to the lowly soul
  Doth still Himself impart,
And for His dwelling and His throne
  Chooseth the pure in heart.

Lord, we Thy presence seek,
  May ours this blessing be:
Give us a pure and lowly heart,
  A temple meet for Thee.

Thursday.

OUR WORDS.

TEXT: PROV. XVIII. 2.

'Death and life are in the power of the tongue.'

'DEATH and life,' does the wise man say? What a strong weapon then for good or for evil your tongue must be!

God has armed you with it. What use do you make of it?

He will ask that question of you one day, and on the answer your whole future will depend; for Christ has said, 'By thy words thou shalt be justified, and by thy words thou shalt be condemned.'

When you carry a loaded gun you are careful how you handle it, lest, touching the trigger carelessly, it should go off and wound the bystanders.

Your tongue is such a loaded gun. By your words you may destroy or save a human soul.

God gave it you to use against His

enemies, the world, the flesh and the devil; do you use it for fighting His battles, or do you turn it against God the giver?

Every time your tongue utters an oath, you are doing the devil's work with it, and not God's.

Every time you use impure, foul language, you are on the side of the devil's legions, not on the side of Christ.

Every time you say the thing which is not, you are fighting for the father of lies instead of for your heavenly Father.

Better to be born dumb than use your tongue in such a service.

How can you use it for Christ to-day? By standing up like a brave man for God and goodness, among your mates at work. By speaking out when you hear them use bad words and checking it by your speech and example. By telling others of the love of Jesus, of the worth of their precious souls, and of the awfulness of eternity. And above all, by using your tongue for praise as the angels do; for prayer as God's saints do.

You can make no nobler use of your tongue than that, for thus it becomes God's instrument in showing forth His glory, and in helping your fellow-men.

You are the sworn soldier of Jesus: do

not be found to-day fighting on the wrong side.

Pray to God and say: Open Thou my lips, O Lord, and my mouth shall show forth Thy praise.

Prayer.

O Father Almighty, who art the giver of every good and perfect gift, grant me grace to use them all to Thy glory.

Thou seest how easily my tongue betrays me into sin, how hard it is to speak the truth at all times, to stand up bravely for Thee and to keep my mouth as it were with bridle, that no foul or evil words may come forth from my lips: oh, be with me as I go forth to my work to-day.

Preserve me from saying one word which I dare not repeat before Thy judgment-seat. Help me to remember that for every idle word I must one day give an account, and let no swearing or cursing, no impure conversation, or light jests, be the means of my leading others into sin.

Set a watch, O Lord, before my mouth, and keep the door of my lips that I offend not with my tongue, and teach me so to train it here to prayer and praise that at last I may stand among the company of the blessed, who

Second Week—Thursday.

sing Thy praise eternally in our heavenly home above.

Hear, O Lord, and answer me, for Jesus' sake. Amen.

Hymn.

The star of morn has risen,
   O Lord, to Thee we pray;
O Uncreated Light of Light,
     Be Thou our day.

Sinless be tongue and hand,
   And innocent the mind;
Let simple truth be on our lips,
     Our words be kind.

As the swift day rolls on,
   Still, Lord, our guardian be;
And keep our daily thoughts and speech
     From evil free.

Grant that our daily toil
   May to Thy glory tend;
And as our hours begin with Thee,
     So may they end.

Friday.

TEMPERANCE.

TEXT: PROV. XXIII. 31, 32.

'Look not thou on the wine when it is red, when it giveth its colour in the cup, when it moveth itself aright. At the last it biteth like a serpent, and stingeth like an adder.'

THERE is an old saying that every man has his price. What that price is, the devil is not slow to find out, for his only aim is to get each of you to sell your souls as cheaply as possible.

Judas sold himself for thirty pieces of silver. Some of you sell your souls for less even than he did.

Many a man strikes a bargain with the devil, unwittingly, at the public-house, and sells his soul then and there for love of drink.

It is not done in a day, but by little and little, for the devil is cautious in making his bargain, for fear lest men should turn back before it is too late, and seeing what fools they have been, ask God to save them from the devil and from their own folly.

Then be warned in time, and never make light of the danger of drink, lest you sell your soul for an extra glass.

A man who begins by 'getting tight' and thinking no shame of it, has struck a bargain with the devil which will cost him more than he dreams of now.

He is taking a serpent to his heart, which has a most deadly sting, and sooner or later he will bitterly rue it.

Go to our great gaols, ask what fills them with prisoners; out of one thousand men and women in one of them, 879 were there for crimes committed when they were in drink. Is that no serpent's sting?

Ask in our large pauper lunatic asylums what brings most madmen there; out of every hundred men in one of them eighty-seven were maddened by drink. Is that no devil's sting?

I do not ask you to take the pledge, or never to touch beer, though Heaven knows in face of such frightful danger it were not wholly unreasonable. But this I do pray and entreat you, learn to be masters of yourselves.

Stop at the first glass which leaves you less of a man than you were before you drank it.

Temperance.

Deny yourselves, lest your example should encourage others to go into temptation. Turn away from the public-house or from the gin-shop where your earnings will go in forming bad habits, in getting accustomed to the sight of sin.

And never, by word or jest, laugh at those of your companions who have put themselves in the devil's clutches.

How can a drunken man be an object of ridicule? God and His angels look on in grief and anger to see a man so defile himself; will you laugh at it?

Rather turn away and pray, remembering that 'drunkards shall not inherit the kingdom of God.'

Let not the devil triumph by man's sin, but strive both to live a temperate, sober life yourself, and do all in your power to help others to do so too.

'For what shall it profit a man if he gain the whole world and lose his own soul? or, what shall a man give in exchange for his soul?'

Prayer.

O Lord God, who seest our weakness and feebleness, save us from the devil's snares. We have been bought with a price, even with the precious blood of Christ our

Lord. Let us not sell ourselves to the devil.

Save us from the love of drink; save us from the temptation of making light of evil.

Have mercy on those who have gone astray, and who by drunkenness have fallen into crime; give them grace, O Lord, to repent before the door of mercy is quite shut against them, and deliver them from the power of sin.

Help us, Lord, by word, by example, and by our prayers, to fight against the cursed love of drink which is the ruin of so many souls.

Bless all those who are fighting the great battle of temperance for Thee amongst our fellow-men, and make us Thy faithful soldiers always more than conquerors for Jesus' sake, our Lord. Amen.

Saturday.

HONESTY.

Text: Rom. xii. 17.

'Provide things honest in the sight of all men.'

There are two bad D's which bring young fellows like you into trouble.

One is drink, the other is debt, and the first leads to the second.

A man who goes often to the public-house is pretty sure to leave most of his wages there, and run up scores elsewhere for food and clothing because he has spent on drink the money which ought to have paid for them.

Have you remembered the text? If not, stop and think about it.

To-day is Saturday—pay day. What use are you going to make of your wages to-night?

The text lays down a pretty clear rule for you. It says, Be honest with every one. Give to every man his due.

Did it ever strike you that debt was a

kind of dishonesty? A man who runs up bills and does not pay them, is putting his hand into the tradesman's pocket just as much as if he stole his purse.

Perhaps you have prided yourself on being an honest man, and never thought of debt in this light. You only said to yourself that it was very hard to be poor, and rather pitied yourself for having a long bill staring you in the face.

But how was that bill run up? Was it because you preferred spending in tobacco and beer the money which ought to have gone towards paying it?

A man who acts thus is dishonourable, be he gentleman or workman.

If you want to be an honest man, it is not enough 'to keep your hands from picking and stealing,' you must also 'be true and just in all your dealings,' in spending your wages, as well as in earning them.

You may have heard some debts spoken of as 'debts of honour.' It is a misleading name. For all debts are debts of honour. A man furnishes you with a certain amount of goods on the understanding that you will give him an equal value in money; if you fail to do so, you have broken faith with him. Is not that dishonourable? You have taken his property and deceived him into the bargain. A thief can hardly do more.

A man who gets into debt not only wrongs his neighbour, but wrongs himself. He is his own worst enemy; for he is fastening the first links of a chain round his neck, which will clog his footsteps every year more and more.

Then remember the good old proverb, 'Out of debt out of danger,' and resolve in this, as in all other things, to 'provide things honest in the sight of all men.'

Prayer.

O Lord God, who hast bid me love my neighbour as myself, and do to all men as I would they should do to me, make me honest in all my dealings.

Keep me from wronging any one by word or deed. Make me a faithful servant to my earthly master, remembering that I have a Master in heaven to whom I must one day give an account.

Help me to spend wisely and well the talent with which Thou hast entrusted me, not squandering my money in wrong or foolish ways, but using it as Thy servant and in Thy service.

Teach me always to provide things honest in the sight of all men, that I may walk before

Honesty.

Thee in my integrity here, and be with Thee for ever hereafter.

Lord, hear my prayer for Jesus Christ's sake. Amen.

HYMN.

Be thrifty, yet not covetous: therefore give
    Thy need, thy honour, and thy friend his due.
Never was scraper a brave man. Get to live,
    Then live and use it; else it is not true
That thou hast gotten. Surely use alone
Makes money not a contemptible stone.

By no means run in debt; take thine own measure;
    Who cannot live on twenty pounds a-year,
Cannot on forty. He's a man of pleasure,
    A kind of thing that's for itself too dear.
The curious unthrift makes his clothes too wide,
And spares himself and would his tailor chide.

THIRD WEEK.

Sunday.

CHURCH BELLS.

TEXT: EXOD. XXXI. 15.

'Six days may work be done, but the seventh is the Sabbath of rest, holy to the Lord.'

WHAT do you do with your Sundays? To a working man they ought to be steps on the ladder to heaven.

You have not much time on week days to yourself. You go off to your work early and come home late, tired out. Because God would not have you too tired to think of Him, He gives you your Sundays, on which He says, 'Rest and be thankful.' Put away the thought of your business, and think of your soul. Shut out earth and let in heaven. Leave the dusty road of your working days, and rest by the waters of life.

And men answer God and say, 'I will rest, but it shall be by lying in bed half the day, and after that I will have my pipe, standing at the public-house, and watching the others go to church. A glass of beer is worth more to me than a prayer. The police reports are more amusing than my Bible.'

Does this shock you? You do not *say* the words, but you *live* them; which is worst?

For every man there are but two futures possible,—heaven or hell. Your present life is so far away from heaven, that were God to take you to His holy home when you die, you would be miserable.

And hell,—who wishes to share in that sorrowful outer darkness?

O my friends, what sort of life is this that you are choosing, and whither are you drifting with such light-hearted carelessness? Let the Sunday church bells be to you a reproach and a reminder. God has better pleasures in store for you than these of your present choosing. This life is but the beginning of our real life. Will you throw away all your fortune at the first cast?

You are more foolish than a child lighting a candle with a 100,000*l*. Bank of England note. For if you throw away your chance in this life, you make yourself a bankrupt for eternity.

You have staked your all, and the devil has won.

His one aim is to blind you to the life beyond the grave, to make you believe in no future, to care for nothing but the present; that so, hiding from your sight the crown of heavenly jewels which God holds out, you may value more the dust-heaps of the devil's offering.

Go on raking it together now. Some day, when it is too late, you will find that there is a life in which a prayer would be more to you than a glass of beer, and one Bible promise better than all your newspapers.

Oh, why will you not believe it now, and listen to Jesus Christ this Sunday, when He says,—'Come unto me, and I will give you rest'?

Prayer.

Lord, have mercy on us, miserable sinners, who turn away from Thee for such vile and petty pleasures. O Christ, have pity on our madness and folly, and open our eyes before it is too late. Thou who didst give Thy life for us, that we might be saved and live, teach us how to spend our days on earth that we may be made fit for the joys of heaven. Raise our hearts and our hopes to Thee, that sin may be a real pain and agony to us;

that we may shun it, hate it, and conquer it; and that loving God and goodness above all things, we may look forward with burning longing for the life of the world to come, for Jesus' sake. Amen.

Hymn.

This is the day of light:
  Let there be light to-day,
O Dayspring, rise upon our night
  And chase its gloom away!

This is the day of rest:
  Our failing strength renew;
On weary brain and troubled breast
  Shed Thou Thy freshening dew.

This is the day of peace:
  Thy peace our spirits fill;
Bid Thou the blasts of discord cease,
  The waves of strife be still.

This is the day of prayer:
  Let earth and heaven draw near;
Lift up our hearts to seek Thee there,
  Come down to meet us here.

This is The first of days:
  Send forth Thy quickening breath,
And wake dead souls to love and praise,
  Thou Vanquisher of death.

Monday.

COURAGE.

TEXT: PROV. XXVIII. 1.

'The righteous are as bold as a lion.'

ENGLISHMEN pride themselves a great deal on their courage, and perhaps rightly so. Whether the danger to be faced were on the stormy seas, or amidst the roar of battle, Englishmen have stood firm, and dared where other men were daunted. They have not flinched from death: they have flinched from being branded with the name of a coward.

It is a grand thing to be brave, but the every-day courage of doing your duty is the grandest courage of all.

If you would be brave with that courage, you must learn to face what is difficult and unpleasant, to bear what is painful, to conquer what is sinful.

God gives to every man his work. He who shrinks from any part of that daily task is a coward.

Your work to-day may be to silence some evil tongue, to defend right against wrong, to oppose impurity with purity, to hold up God's truth against a lie. It is sometimes harder for a young fellow to face such work and do it courageously than it is to face an earthly foe.

The pain of being laughed at, despised, and shunned by your fellow-workmen, is keener than the wound of a bayonet thrust. The difficulty of always doing right, and standing up for it day by day, is harder work than storming an enemy's stronghold under fire, or forcing your way through the ranks of the foe.

But if you are a Christian, you may not shirk God's orders because they are difficult, or refuse to obey because you are afraid of the consequences. You must obey at all costs.

Obedience to right is the first law of a Christian's life. He who shrinks from it is a coward, and shall receive a coward's doom.

Remember also that every unpleasant duty you turn from to-day, will make the next one harder to face. Every difficulty you set down as hopeless, will make you more despairing for the future. Every pain you refuse to bear will make you more impatient of suffering, and unnerve you for the next trial.

Every cowardice will make you more and more cowardly, till at last you become a contemptible being, unworthy of your Christian manhood, of your Christian prize.

Then take God's orders as given to you in His holy word, and stand by them to the death. You are going forth to your daily work this morning. You are on your trial as a brave man or a coward. Do not be found wanting. 'Be very courageous, and the Lord your God shall be with you for good.'

Prayer.

O Lord our God, who givest strength unto those who ask it of Thee, I pray give me courage to-day to do my work bravely for Thee. Lord, Thou knowest how weak and cowardly we are, how easily the fear of man turns us aside from the path of duty. Fill me with the fear of Thee alone, that I may dread nothing so much as evil, and shun nothing so much as being found cowardly in doing Thy work. Give me grace to rebuke sin, to suffer patiently for the truth's sake, and to overcome pain and difficulty. Make me ever valiant in Thy cause, that I may never turn my back on the enemy; but that fulfilling all Thy commands without flinching, I may at last attain to everlasting life, through the merits of Jesus Christ, my only Lord and Saviour. Amen.

Courage.

HYMN.

Stand up, stand up for Jesus,
   Ye soldiers of the cross;
Lift high His royal banner,
   Ye may not suffer loss.
From victory unto victory
   His servants shall He lead,
Till every foe be vanquished,
   And Christ be Lord indeed.

Stand up, stand up for Jesus,
   The fight will not be long;
To-day the noise of battle,
   The next, the victor's song.
To him that overcometh,
   The prize of joy shall be;
And he, with Christ, for ever
   Shall reign in victory.

Tuesday.

TRUTH.

TEXT: Ps. cxx. 2.

'Deliver my soul, O Lord, from lying lips, and from a deceitful tongue.'

It is said that the ancient Persians taught their sons three things: to ride, to shoot, and to speak the truth. When a boy had learnt that, they thought his education was complete.

In at least one of these three things they were right: for the first lesson of a man's life is to be true. Till you have learnt that, you have learnt nothing. Truth is a firm rock on which you may build up the other virtues. Without it, all your trouble will be in vain.

A man whose life is a lie is nothing but a miserable sham of manhood. There is no greatness possible where there is no truth.

Some people fancy by cunning and deceit

to get on in the world. They think themselves sharp for being able to take others in, and call it doing a good stroke of business. Lies come as glibly to their tongue as though it were their interest never to speak the truth. They weigh out their souls for the devil's gold, and men call them prosperous.

Is it prospering to damn yourself?

If you could look into your soul and see what a foul, black stain that 'white lie' has just made there, you would turn away with loathing and despair.

Better be a poor man all your life than buy a fortune with one lie. Better go hungry all your days than buy the devil's bread by earning his wages.

Once learn what a precious thing truth is, and you will be able to sacrifice wages, employment, love, aye, and happiness, rather than soil your hands and heart by insincerity.

You are a working man, but keep your soul clean. Let it be your pride to make your whole life so transparently pure and true, that men may trust your word as though it were a king's.

Let it be said of you, as it was once of a great ruler, that your word is as good as another man's bond.

And remember always that a man may lie by his silence, as much as by his speech.

Third Week—Tuesday.

He may lie by concealing the truth as much as by denying it. By whatever means you wilfully make another believe the thing which is not, you are so far lying to him.

It will cost you much to be always true, but the truth is well purchased at any price. You are going off to your work. Do not forget it to-day. 'Buy the truth and sell it not.'

Prayer.

O Christ, who art the Truth, lead me in Thy way of perfect truth. Save me from cheating, 'white lies,' and all insincerity of word or deed. Make me so trustworthy that men may know me to be a child of light, and a follower of Jesus Christ. Set a watch, Lord, before my mouth, and keep the door of my lips, that I offend not with my tongue. Keep me always in Thy presence, that I may not dare to lie unto Thee, who searchest the reins and the heart, and who punishest liars in the lake which burns with fire. Teach me to hate lies even as Thou hatest them, that so walking before Thee with clean hands and a pure heart, I may be received at last into that blessed home which nothing defiled shall enter, for Thy Love's sake. Amen.

Wednesday.

THE POWER OF EXAMPLE.

TEXT: GEN. IV. 9.

'And the Lord said unto Cain, Where is Abel thy brother? And he said, I know not: am I my brother's keeper?'

WHAT was the true answer to God's question? Abel's corpse lay cold and stiff in the open field, slain by a brother's hand. Cain was his murderer.

There are two kinds of murder. Murder of the body and murder of the soul. Murderers of the body suffer death by the law of their country. Do murderers of the soul escape all punishment, think you? God punishes them.

It is a terrible thing to murder a soul. Have you ever considered what it means?

The devil is the great soul murderer. It is his trade to murder souls. But men help him in it.

God has said the 'wages of sin is death.'

Every time you lead others into sin you are helping to murder their souls. You are holding out the poison cup, and bidding your brother drink of it. You may say, He needn't copy me unless he likes; I didn't ask him to follow me into the public-house and get drunk, or tell him to poach, to lie, to steal, because I do it. It's his own look out.' Aye, you murder your brother by your evil deeds, and then ask with Cain, 'Am I my brother's keeper?' But God's answer will still be the same, 'What is this that thou hast done? The voice of thy brother's blood crieth unto me from the ground.' And upon you will fall the curse, as it did upon Cain.

God gave you the power of setting others a noble example of honesty, temperance, uprightness, holiness. Instead of doing so, you spent your life in wickedness, in drunkenness, in deceit, in dishonesty. Not only do you ruin your own soul, but you drag down others with you. The young brother who thought it manly to copy you; the weak companion who worked at your side, and who had not the courage to say 'No,' to you, when you laughed at him for being a saint, these will meet you again at the Judgment-seat, and standing before God condemned, turn to you and say, 'You helped to bring me to *this*.'

God save us all from such a terrible meeting! God give us grace now, while there is time, to help men in doing what is right, to stand up boldly both by word and example for religion and goodness, and to lead others on the way to heaven, that so our lives may be a blessing to our fellow-men and not a curse.

For, remember, there is no getting out of it. Your example must tell one way or another, for Christ or for the devil.

For heaven or for hell—which shall it be to-day?

Prayer.

O Lord Jesus, who hast taught us the danger and wickedness of breaking one of the least of Thy commandments and teaching men so, save me to-day from being in any way a stumbling-block to one of Thy disciples. When I go out to my work make me careful both of my words and of my actions, lest I should encourage others to do wrong. Help me to bear Thy holy presence always in mind, that when temptation comes I may say with Joseph, 'How can I do this great wickedness, and sin against God?' Make me pure and holy, sober and industrious, and be with me now and always, for Thy love's sake. Amen.

Hymn.

We scatter seeds with careless hand,
    And dream we ne'er shall see them more:
        But for a thousand years
        Their fruit appears,
In weeds that mar the land,
    Or healthful store.

The deeds we do, the words we say,
    Into still air they seem to fleet;
        We count them ever past,
        But they shall last:
In the dread judgment they
    And we shall meet.

I charge thee by the years gone by,
    For the love's sake of brethren dear,
        Keep thou the one true way
        In work and play,
Lest in that world their cry
    Of woe thou hear.

Thursday.

FRIENDS.

Text: St. John, xv. 15.

'I have called you friends.'

It has been said, 'Tell me who a man's friends are, and I will tell you what he is.' A man's life depends so much on the kind of friendships he makes.

Every man has one Friend by whom he should try all others: that Friend is Jesus Christ. You can have no unworthy friendships if you let Him choose them for you.

He has bound together all who love Him in one golden chain of union. He says of them, 'I have called you friends.' Are the friends of Christ your friends too? Does the mere fact of a man being a Christian attach you more warmly to him?

We say in church, 'I believe in the communion of saints.' You must show that belief by your life. It is only real to a Christian man.

To him it is a constant reminder of his friends in earth and heaven. When he is lonely, the remembrance of the saints in paradise whose life is one long praise, and of the saints on earth whose life is one long fight, comforts and supports him. He is one of a glorious band of friends, one in the 'great family' of earth and heaven; he cannot be forlorn.

If you have chosen the friends of Christ to be yours, you will try to be like them. Christ's friends have the same interests, the same aims. They are all looking forward to their home in heaven: all hoping for the time when they shall be with Christ for ever. Whether their work be behind the counter or in the field, in the factory or the workshop, all they do is a preparation for home. Your friends and you will talk of it, long for it, live for it.

You do not care to talk of home to strangers. If you make earthly friends of wild careless fellows who never look beyond to-day, never think of Christ your Friend, all your thoughts and ways will be strange to them. They will neither understand nor care for the things which fill your heart.

And the danger to you will be just this; that by degrees you will get to care less for the heavenly Friend you cannot see, and more for the worldly ones who will lead you away from your best Friend, Jesus Christ.

'Be not deceived,' says St. Paul; 'evil communications corrupt good manners.' It is easy to begin a friendship, hard to break away from it, when it has become a pleasant custom.

Then take Jesus Christ into your confidence. Ask Him to make all your friendships noble, pure, and loyal ones, remembering always that a man which hath friends must 'show himself friendly;' but there is 'a Friend which sticketh closer than a brother.' Earthly friendships are beautiful, but the perfection of true friendship is only found in heaven.

Prayer.

O Lord Jesus, who art the Friend of all Thy faithful servants, teach me to lean entirely on Thee. Earthly friends may fail me, but Thou, Lord, wilt never leave or forsake me.

Choose Thou all my friendships for me, O Lord, that I may not make friends of Thine enemies, or be led away by the voice of worldly, careless people to do wrong and forget Thy loving counsels.

And, O Lord, teach me to be a good friend to others: make me loyal, staunch, and true; help me to be really unselfish, putting my friends first always, and trying to help them upwards on the road to heaven: that so we may be linked together by ties which never can be broken, even in death, and may spend a happy eternity in the home beyond, where Thy friends shall walk for ever in the light of Thy countenance.

Lord, hear my prayer, for Thy Love's sake. Amen.

Hymn.

Come let us join our friends above
    Who have obtained the prize,
And on the eagle wings of love
    To joys celestial rise.

Let saints on earth in concert sing
    With those whose work is done;
For all the servants of our King
    In heaven and earth are one.

One family we dwell in Him,
    One church, above, beneath:
Though now divided by the stream—
    The narrow stream of death.

One army of the living God,
    To His command we bow;
Part of the host have crossed the flood,
    And part are crossing now.

Friends.

Lord Jesu, be our constant Guide,
 Then when the word is given,
Bid death's cold stream its waves divide,
 And land us safe in heaven.

Friday.

HONOUR.

Text: St. John, v. 44.

'The honour which cometh from God only.'

This is the honour of a Christian man. Make it your standard in life, and your honour will be on a firm footing. For what is disgrace? I suppose being made worse than you were.

And that lies entirely in your own power. No man can force you to do wrong. You have a will: use it, and will to do right always.

If you let your honour rest on men's opinion of you merely, you will lose all right to the name of an honourable man. You may have stained your soul, and men be none the wiser; but are you not disgraced? 'Before no man be so shamefaced as before thyself.'

Let God and your conscience be your judges, and obey them in the smallest things.

Honour.

Every act has a right and a wrong. The wrong is dishonour.

An honourable man is one who cannot stoop to defile himself: one who is never turned aside from duty, by pleasure or interest: one who keeps his eyes fixed on the white aim, and whose arrows fly straight home to it. Men may laugh or sneer, frown or praise; he does not look to them but to God as the judge of all he does. So you will find his work true and good, whether it is done under the master's eye or behind his back. There is no shirking, no sham, in his life. It is brave, simple, faithful, all of a piece. When God looks at your life, will He find it like this?

If you learn to look upon sin as the only disgrace, you will jealously guard your soul from every blot of untruthfulness, impurity, irreverence. You will try to keep clean hands and a pure heart, to shut out bad thoughts, to live a higher life than your comrades. You will never say, 'It doesn't matter; it's no such great sin after all,' for all wrong-doing will be pain.

And such a life will tell on your companions also. No man was ever better himself without making others the better for it. A high standard raises others. It makes them ashamed of their cowardly yielding to temptation. One brave man has sometimes stopped a regiment from flight. They could not desert him entirely, and seeing him face the enemy so calmly, they gained courage for another onset. That is your work for Jesus Christ; by seeking the honour which comes from God only, to make others ashamed of caring so much about what the neighbours say; by standing up for truth, purity, and self-control, to make others long to purify themselves, even as Christ is pure; by your upright, noble life, to straighten the crooked lives around you. It is a grand work, and God will bless it. For He says, 'Them that honour Me, I will honour; but those that despise Me shall be lightly esteemed.'

Prayer.

O Lord our God, who hast taught that true honour comes only from Thee, and belongs to those who follow Thy commandments, make me to look on sin as the only real disgrace. Wash me from every stain, give me clean hands and a pure heart, that I may walk before Thee in uprightness, and live a holy, blameless life.

Let me never fall below Thy standard, or follow any example save that of my Master Christ. Keep me from being turned aside by the fear of man, by the evil opinion of others, or by the dislike of seeming singular. Give me grace to confess Thee before my fellow-men, and to be loyal to my belief in Thee, that so I may be among those who by patient continuance in well-doing, seeking glory, honour, immortality, shall obtain eternal life through Jesus Christ our Lord. Amen.

HYMN.

How happy is he born and taught,
    Who serveth not another's will;
Whose armour is his honest thought,
    And simple truth his utmost skill;

Whose passions not his masters are,
    Whose soul is still prepared for death,
Not tied unto the world with care
    Of public fame or private breath.

Who envies none that chance doth raise,
    Or vice; who never understands
How deepest wounds are given by praise;
    Not rules of state but rules of good:

Who hath his life from rumours freed,
    Whose conscience is his strong retreat;
Whose state can neither flatterers feed,
    Nor ruin make accusers great.

Third Week—Friday.

Who God doth late and early pray
    More of His grace than gifts to lend,
And entertains the harmless day
    With a well-chosen book or friend.

This man is free from servile bands
    Of hope to rise, or fear to fall;
Lord of himself, though not of lands,
    And having nothing, yet hath all.

Saturday.

STRENGTH.

TEXT: PROV. xx. 29.

'The glory of young men is their strength.'

How may your strength prove your glory?

The brutes are strong in muscle and sinew. That is not enough for a Christian man. Brute force is not manliness.

There is a strength of body and there is a strength of soul.

Samson was strong in one way. St. John the Baptist was strong in the other. Which was the most glorious life?

Samson carried away the iron gates of Gaza on his shoulder, and slew a lion with nothing in his hand: but when temptation met him he was weak as a child. A woman conquered him.

How did such strength profit him?

St. John the Baptist was strong in a nobler way. He stood his ground without flinching, for the sake of God and right.

Neither a dungeon nor death could make him afraid to do his duty. He was strong to do battle with wrong, strong to uphold the truth, strong to bear pain rather than let the devil conquer him. He braved men's blame, men's hatred, men's persecution, because God and goodness were worth more to him than any earthly glory; exile and death were no evils to him, because his heart and conscience were at peace. And so his strength made even the king fear him. Men quailed before that stern standard which knew but two words —right or wrong. His fortitude made them ashamed of their weakness, their cowardice.

Strength of soul is hard to attain. We all shrink from pain, from punishment, from scorn. Yet unless you gain that strength, that fortitude, you will never know true manliness.

Fortitude is the knowing what things ought to be feared.

It is the replacing of an ignorant fear by a noble one—a fear of giving up truth, a fear of defiling and lowering yourself, a fear of growing down like the devils, instead of upwards like the angels.

When such a fear enters a man's life, men call it fortitude; because in comparison with the evils they dread, these evils become to you far worse ones.

You can bear being laughed at, being taunted, being scorned. You cannot bear to do wrong.

Such a life is true strength, true glory, but it will cost you much to live it. You may be left alone, deserted by your friends, with but little encouragement anywhere to persevere in this grave steadfastness. You will be like one who has climbed the mountains, and left the rest below: but in the silence of that height you will find God, and raise others, perchance, to a nobler standard, if it be but by awakening shame and showing them the possible.

Such a life is worth living for, worth dying for. Will you strive after it to-day?

'Finally, my brethren, be strong in the Lord, and in the power of His might.'

Prayer.

O Lord, Almighty God, who hast promised that 'they which wait upon the Lord shall renew their strength,' make my soul strong for Thy service. Keep me from putting bodily strength before strength of soul. Make me more thoroughly in earnest, that I may love God and right above all things, and never fear the face of man. Help me to do battle with evil, with sloth, with difficulty, that in

Third Week—Saturday.

all my work, and through my whole life, I may strive to attain the glory which comes from Thee. Fill my soul with a noble strength and courage, and be with me, now and evermore, for Jesus' sake. Amen.

Hymn.

Fight the good fight with all thy might,
Christ is thy strength and Christ thy right;
Lay hold on life, and it shall be
Thy joy and crown eternally.

Run the straight race through God's good grace,
Lift up thine eyes and seek His Face;
Life with its way before thee lies:
Christ is the path, and Christ the prize.

Cast care aside, lean on thy Guide,
His boundless mercy will provide;
Lean, and the trusting soul shall prove
Christ is its life and Christ its love.

Faint not, nor fear; His arms are near;
He changeth not, and Thou art dear:
Only believe, and thou shalt see
That Christ is all in all to thee.

FOURTH WEEK.

Sunday.

THE BREAD OF LIFE.

Text: St. John, vi. 54.

'Whoso eateth my flesh, and drinketh my blood, hath eternal life, and I will raise him up at the last day.'

To-day is the feast of the resurrection—the day on which Christ Jesus our Lord conquered death for us, and opened out life eternal for His people.

Death was a terrible thing before. To the heathen it was a dark shadow which filled their lives with gloom. In the midst of their feasting and their most riotous joy, the thought of death was like a skeleton at their side, grim, cruel, not to be chased away. The cold, dark grave, which put an end to all that they found pleasant and beautiful in this life, was constantly before them; their songs, their books, are all full of it. 'Only give us some hope of a happy future,' they cry, 'else this life is unbearable.'

What a blessed thing the gospel was to them. It 'brought life and immortality to light.' Henceforth death was only the gate to a far brighter, more glorious life, by the side of which their happiest days here were sorrowful.

Have you ever thought of death? Are you afraid of it?

There is only one remedy for your fear. Have you accepted that remedy?

Jesus gives life; Jesus saves from death. As long as you keep away from Jesus Christ, you may well fear death. Only in Him is life; only He can save you from death eternal.

And He tells you how: by coming to Him, and asking Him for that gift of eternal life.

While you are on earth you can come to Him in two ways only; by prayer, and by the Holy Communion.

Have you obeyed His call? Do you come to Him as He bids you?

Many young fellows keep away from that holy feast because they think they are not good enough.

Jesus Christ says, 'Come.'

The Bread of Life.

He does not ask if you are good enough. No one, not even the greatest saint, can be that. He asks if you are really sorry for sin, and if you truly desire to be made better. To such He says, 'Him that cometh unto Me, I will in no wise cast out.'

Go to Him to-day.

Others stay away because they think they will have to lead a stricter life afterwards. That is surely a strange delusion. Christ says to every one, 'Be ye therefore perfect, even as your Father which is in heaven is perfect.' He knows no lower standard for any Christian man to aim at.

But he never leaves us to work by ourselves. So He has ordained this most blessed feast to strengthen us by uniting us to Him, and by His grace leading us upwards.

When you stay away from it, you lose all possible chance of getting holier and better, and you are still bound to that high standard of perfection.

For wilful disobedience there is a terrible penalty. Will you risk it?

Keeping away from Jesus Christ means death to your soul. 'Except ye eat the flesh of the Son of Man and drink His blood, ye have no life in you.'

Think of it when you turn away and go out of church. Think of the prize you miss, the grace you lose. Let not Christ our Lord say sorrowfully of you as of the Jews of old, 'Ye will not come unto me that ye might have life.'

Prayer.

O Lord Jesus, the conqueror of death, and the Saviour of men, give unto me, I beseech Thee, Thy great gift of eternal life. Lord, if I am Thine, I need not fear death, because in Thee I shall live again a happier, holier life than this earthly one; but without Thee I must die eternally. Save, Lord, or I perish. Lord, Thou hast bid me come to Thee in the Holy Communion of Thy body and blood; but I am very weak and sinful, and I hardly dare to approach Thee. Lord, strengthen my weakness, cleanse me from my sin, and make me a worthy receiver of Thine unspeakable gift. Only in Thee I can grow strong to resist sin, strong to live a pure, manly life. Lord, pour Thy grace upon me, that my week-day life may not be a reproach to my Sunday profession, but that obeying Thee faithfully here in all things, I may be saved from death and brought to the life eternal, for Thy love's sake, because Thou hast died for me. Amen.

The Bread of Life.

Hymn.

We come to Thee, dear Saviour,
   Just because we need Thee so.
None need Thee more than we do,
   None are half so vile and low.

We come to Thee, dear Saviour,
   With our broken faith again;
We know Thou wilt forgive us,
   Nor upbraid us nor complain.

We come to Thee, dear Saviour,
   It is love that makes us come:
We are certain of our welcome,—
   Of our Father's weltome home.

We come to Thee, dear Saviour,
   Fear brings us in our need;
For Thy hand never breaketh
   E'en the frailest bruised reed.

We come to Thee, dear Saviour,
   For to whom, Lord, can we go?
The words of life eternal
   From Thy lips ever flow.

We come to Thee, dear Saviour,
   And Thou wilt not ask us why;
We cannot live without Thee,
   And still less without Thee die.

Monday.

GENTLENESS.

TEXT: 2 TIM. II. 24.

'The servant of the Lord must not strive, but be gentle unto all men.'

A GENTLEMAN or a rough—which would you rather be?

The text tells you which God means all His children to be—gentlemen.

But you are a working man; how can you be one?

Perhaps you think it depends on money and position. Many a man with 10,000*l.* a-year is nothing but a rough. That has not much to do with it. You must go deeper if you want to know what God means.

Real refinement comes straight from the heart: it is born of unselfish love. Is that beyond the reach of a working man?

As one of God's sons, you dare not fall below your Father's standard of Christian gentleness.

Gentleness.

How then can you reach it, and so learn to be one of His gentlemen? I think by having much feeling for the rest of the world, as well as for yourself—by always putting others first, and avoiding what would wound or hurt them. By forgetting your own rights that you may give others their due; by thinking much of the weak, the sorrowful, the unprotected, and using your strength to help their feebleness.

Gentleness will not let you elbow your way through the world, careless who goes to the wall, if only you can push your way forward.

It will make you keep your temper when you are rudely spoken of, or provoked, and silence the oath or the blow which would be your natural answer.

Gentleness is not womanish, but the truest Christian manliness. Look at the example of our Master, when He stood before the Council, and one of them which stood by struck Him on the mouth. He might have answered the blow by a word which would have been death. What *did* He do? 'Jesus answered him, If I have spoken evil, bear witness of the evil; but if well, why smitest thou me?' Will you imitate that noble gentleness which nothing could ever ruffle or tire?

Fourth Week—Monday.

A gentleman shows his breeding in his words, his manners, his voice, as well as his acts. If you are a son of God, you cannot be rude, rough, ill-tempered. You will show your heavenly rank in all you do or say. You will learn to keep yourself well in hand, lest you should disgrace your heavenly parentage, and cause men to speak slightingly of God's children. For His dear sake you will remember that 'the servant of the Lord *must* be gentle unto all men.'

Try and practise it, then, in little things to-day: by your silence as well as by your talk: by your thoughts as well as by your acts. So, though a working man, you will become a true Christian gentleman, and learn the meaning of King David's words, when he said of God, his Heavenly Father, 'Thy gentleness hath made me great.'

PRAYER.

O God, our Father, who hast made us Thy sons, teach me to be worthy of my Christian rank. Make me gentle in all I do and say. Help me to think more of others than of myself; to put them first, and by loving unselfishness to be a blessing and a help to my fellow-men. Make me learn of Christ my Lord, who was meek and lowly of

Gentleness.

heart, that so copying that pattern of heavenly gentleness, I may find rest and peace, so that men may know by my life whose I am, and whom I serve. When I go out to my work to-day, help me to keep Thy command in mind. Check in me every angry, rude word, every harsh, provoking speech, every rough, selfish action, and make me a true Christian gentleman, for Jesus' sake. Amen.

HYMN.

Speak gently, it is better far
  To rule by love than fear.
Speak gently, let not harsh words mar
  The good we might do here.

Speak gently, love doth whisper low
  The vows that true hearts bind,
And gently friendship's accents flow;
  Affection's voice is kind.

Speak gently to the young, for they
  Will have enough to bear;
Pass through this life as best they may,
  'Tis full of anxious care.

Speak gently to the aged one!
  Grieve not the careworn heart;
The sands of life are nearly run,
  Let such in peace depart.

Fourth Week—Monday.

Speak gently to the erring, know
  They may have toiled in vain.
Perchance unkindness made them so.
  Oh, win them back again!

Speak gently! He who gave His life
  To bend man's stubborn will,
When elements were in fierce strife,
  Said to them, 'Peace, be still.'

Speak gently! 'tis a little thing
  Dropped in the heart's deep well!
The good, the joy, that it may bring,
  Eternity shall tell.

Tuesday.

THE FAVOURITE CORNER.

TEXT: Ps. x. 8.

'He sitteth lurking in the thievish corners of the streets.'

THAT is said of the wicked one—the devil. Do you love to sit by his side?

Every man has his favourite corner, to which he resorts when his work is over. Where is yours? Some young fellows turn to the public-house, and hang about the door, talking to those who go in and out of the gin-palaces; or they go in and sit down with them. They have the devil at their elbow there; they are going into temptation.

Others loaf about at the village corner, where the idle, lazy companions congregate; their loud laughs and rude jokes are heard there late in the evening: some of them are the worse for liquor, and hardly know what they say. They forget that the evil one 'sitteth in the lurking places of the villages.'

The devil's corners are bad ones to be

the favourites of any Christian man. Don't go to them, or make them yours.

More men fall into sin through carelessness than through any intention of doing wrong, or getting into mischief. Keep a sharp look-out, and do not be so easily caught in the devil's traps. Remember that if you truly desire to live a noble, manly life, it is dangerous to keep company with those who laugh at what is bad. You are not strong enough to prevent their doing evil; you will be led away by them, and fall. The society of bad companions is far more likely, at present, to do you harm, than you are to do them good. One drop of water in a bottle of ink does not make the ink white. But one drop of ink in a glass of water does make the water black.

When you stand 'in the way of sinners,' and sit down ' in the seat of the scornful,' it is only too easy to join their 'sprees' for the sake of the fun, and laugh at their frolics, though it is God they mock at. You are excited: you don't stay them to think about the right or wrong, but only about what amuses you. Then you come away, and feel ashamed of yourself. You cannot kneel and pray, you feel such a hypocrite: and you turn away from the Holy Communion, because you are not steady and good enough for it.

So you cut yourself loose from your moorings, and God only knows where men drift to, when they drift away from Him. For the 'thievish corners of the streets,' and the 'lurking places by the villages,' there is but one piece of advice, and that is, 'Avoid it, pass not by it, turn from it, and pass away.' It may not harm you to stand there this time or next, and yet you may owe your ruin to what you learned there, before the day is done.

Prayer.

O Lord Jesus, who hast died to save me from the devil's snares; let me not be caught in the traps which he sets for the souls of men. Make me watchful in little things, that I may not be slowly and surely drawn away from what is good and holy. Keep me from little defilements, little stains, from the company of those whose lives are unclean, and who talk and think lightly of sin. Lord, wash Thou me, so shall I be whiter than snow. Keep me pure and stainless here on earth, that so at the last I may stand among the white-robed company of Thy saints in the blessed home which nothing defiling shall enter.

Hear me, and answer for Thy loving mercy's sake. Amen.

Fourth Week—Tuesday.

HYMN.

How bright these glorious spirits shine!
  Whence all their white array,
How came they to the blissful seats
  Of everlasting day?

Lo, these are they from sufferings great
  Who came to realms of light,
And in the Blood of Christ have washed
  Their robes that shine so bright.

Now with triumphal palms they stand
  Before the throne on high,
And serve the God they love amidst
  The glories of the sky.

His Presence fills each heart with joy,
  Tunes every mouth to sing,
By day, by night, the sacred courts
  With glad hosannas sing.

The Lamb which dwells amidst the throne
  Shall o'er them still preside;
Feed them with nourishment divine,
  And all their footsteps guide.

Midst pastures green He'll feed His flock
  Where living streams appear,
And God the Lord from every eye
  Shall wipe off every tear.

Wednesday.

GOD'S WITNESSES,

TEXT: Ps. cxxxvii. 4.

'How shall we sing the Lord's song in a strange land?'

ALL Christians, as long as they are on earth, are in 'a strange land.' Heaven is our fatherland and our home. We are journeying towards the good land which God our Father has promised us. Our citizenship is in heaven.

So the question of King David is one for every Christian man to answer. You must answer it by your life.

What is meant by singing the Lord's song? It means showing forth His praise. Every time you do right, you are singing the Lord's song. Every time you fall away yourself, or lead others to do wrong, you are forgetting the Lord's song. You are bringing His name into dishonour. You are making those about you think what's the use of a man calling himself a Christian when he's none the better for it.

But when careless, thoughtless people are led by your life to stop and say, 'There's something in religion if it's that which makes this young fellow so brave, and gentle, and honest. I would like to try it, for it's better than my lazy, selfish life after all:' then you have sung the Lord's song of praise rightly. You have learnt the heavenly music yourself, and you are teaching other voices to sing it with you.

There is no grander life than one spent in teaching men to sing the Lord's song with you. But it is hard work, because the devil will be always trying to stop your mouth, and make you sing his song instead.

You sing the devil's praises every time you make sin pleasant and easy to others, every time that you lead them away from their duty, every time you laugh at them for doing right. Such discordant music will be heard in hell; it goes up to God now and brings down His wrath on sinful men. Do not join in the wicked chorus of the devils against God your heavenly Father.

Try to make your life so noble, so simple, so pure, so true, that even your smallest actions may be a note in the Lord's song, chording truly with the song of the blessed angels who sing His praises eternally.

You are starting for your work now.

God's Witnesses.

Whether it be to follow the plough, to measure out groceries behind the counter, to wait at table, to wield the hammer, or to use the trowel. I want your constant thought to-day to be, 'How shall I sing the Lord's song in a strange land?'

Prayer.

O Lord Jesus, who by Thy perfect life on earth hast taught us that even the humblest work may be done to Thy glory, help me never to forget it to-day.

Teach me to make melody in my heart to Thee, that even here I may join in the songs of heaven, and show forth Thy praises. Let none of the devil's discords of sin enter my life. Make me so pure and true that men may take knowledge of me that I have been with Christ, and long also to follow Thee. Keep me from ever leading others into sin by my carelessness or bad example, but with the thought of heaven always before my eyes, make me to live a life of love and goodness, that so at last I may be numbered among Thy chosen ones, and be with Thee for evermore, for Thy love's sake. Amen.

Hymn.

Teach me, my God and King,
  In all things Thee to see:
And what I do in anything
  To do it as for Thee.

A man that looks on glass,
  On it may stay his eye;
Or, if he pleaseth, through it pass
  And then the heaven espy.

All may of Thee partake;
  Nothing can be so mean
Which with this tincture 'for Thy sake,'
  Will not grow bright and clean.

A servant with this clause
  Makes drudgery divine;
Who sweeps a room as for Thy laws,
  Makes that and the action fine.

This is the famous stone,
  Which turneth all to gold;
For that which God doth touch and own
  Cannot for less be told.

Thursday.

REVERENCE.

TEXT: GEN. XXVIII. 16.

'And Jacob awaked out of his sleep: and he said, Surely God was in this place and I knew it not.'

A WISE man once said that reverence is the beginning of all education. God educated Jacob by teaching him, first of all, the lesson of His Presence. That is a lesson that every one of you who want to lead a manly, noble life must learn. Feel God's presence in your every-day life, and learn to be reverent in the face of it.

What is reverence? It is just looking up to some one whom we feel to be better, and purer, and wiser than ourselves. It is a lesson of humility, because it makes us feel our place, how low down it is; how poor, and selfish, and sinful we are beside that greatness, that goodness, that wisdom.

Then seeing the higher model we long to copy it, to raise ourselves to something better than we are now. A reverent spirit is the first step in God's ladder to heaven. I want you to set your foot upon that ladder and climb it day by day.

Besides the reverence that we owe to God, as the All-good, the All-wise, there is another kind of reverence that we owe to our fellow-men. There is no such good lesson to learn while you are young as this one of looking up to those who are older, and wiser, and better than you are. Now-a-days it is too much the fashion for young men to look down on everybody and everything, to think themselves quite good enough, and to be so satisfied with their own ways as not to care to mend them.

Once get into that spirit of contemptuous conceit, and you will go steadily backwards all your life in true manliness, instead of going forwards.

You are like a man in prison who one by one blocks up all his windows which open towards the light and sun till he leaves himself in blind darkness.

It is a sorrowful life which sees nothing good, nothing pure, nothing trustworthy in any one; but it is what all men come to, who are always looking down on their fellow-men, and seeking for what is bad in them, instead of trying to see their good qualities, and reverence what is best in them.

There is hardly any one, if you look at them truly, who is not far better than you are in something, or from whose life you may not learn a pure, holy lesson, only we are so blind and selfish, it comes easier to us to scorn and despise others, than it does to love and admire them.

There is one more kind of reverence that I want you to learn, and that is, reverence for yourself—in other words, self-respect. As the child of God, as the temple of the Holy Ghost, you will then feel that a dirty action, an unclean thought is a blot on your soul; you will try to keep clean hands and a pure heart, because all sin will lower you in your own eyes, and make you despise yourself. It is the highest kind of manliness when a man has learnt to dread no one so much as his own conscience, to fear nothing so much as doing wrong and getting bad.

Reverence for God, reverence for your fellow-men, reverence for yourself, that is the alphabet of religion. Begin learning it to-day.

Prayer.

O Lord Almighty, who by a dream didst teach Thy servant Jacob that Thy presence fills the earth, and that before Thy face all creatures bow and adore, give me, I pray Thee, that true reverence which filled his heart when he awoke and felt Thee near. Take from me, I pray Thee, all self-conceit, and foolish scorn of others. Help me to seek out what is good and noble in every one instead of looking down upon them and despising them. Fill me with the spirit of Thy holy fear that in all temptation I may say with Joseph, 'How shall I do this great wickedness and sin against God?' Teach me to live always in Thy presence here, obeying the voice of conscience and faithful to the call of duty, that so living a noble, manly life on earth, I may be received at last into Thy Home of Peace to be with Thee for evermore.

Lord, hear my prayer, and answer me for Jesus' sake. Amen.

Friday.

GETTING ON.

Text: Phil. iii. 13, 14.

'Forgetting those things which are behind, and reaching forth unto those things which are before, I press towards the mark, for the prize of the high calling of God in Christ Jesus.'

How are you getting on in your Christian race? Every sin is a step backward; every victory over your temptations is a step forward. There is no standing still. Which way are you going?

Time is slipping fast away. The race will soon be over: only those who have pressed bravely forward in spite of pain and difficulty shall receive the heavenly reward. Christ holds out the crown of glory to you. He bids you look to God and heaven, and throw your whole strength into this grand struggle of life. He says, 'To him that overcometh will I grant to sit with me in my throne.' Do not lose the race through sheer carelessness and indifference.

How can you tell whether you are really getting on or no? St. Paul answers that question. He says, 'Examine yourselves whether ye be in the faith; prove your own selves.'

You can only truly know what your professions are worth, by asking yourself every day before you lie down to rest, 'What have I done for God to-day? Has He been my aim, or have I forgotten all about Him?' Then think of your faults, and see whether you have got the better of any of them. Did you pull yourself up sharp, when the angry word or oath was on your lips? Did you turn away from bad company? Did you speak out like a man, and silence the lie, the immodest jest, the mocking jeers; or were you silent, and allowed the devil's arrows to fly home?

Did you help your younger comrades to be brave, and lead them out of temptation, or did you take them into danger? Did you do your work honestly, with all your might, or was it a shambling, slip-shod kind of job, because no one was by to see you, and you did not care how it was done as long as you got the money for it? By these and such-like questions you may know whether you are pressing forward like St. Paul, or shrinking back like a coward.

It may have been only a little slip to-day, but each time you give way you lose ground, and make it harder to stand firm when the same temptation comes again.

A straw is blown about by the wind: a bullet flies straight home. I want your aim to be so true, your strength to be so great that nothing may turn you aside. Then go forth to-day, and with eyes fixed on the goal as a man who knows that on this race life and death depend; 'press towards the mark for the prize.'

Prayer.

O Lord Jesus, who seest that we are weak and feeble, easily daunted in running Thy race, and forgetful of the heavenly crown which Thou dost hold out to us, be with me to-day, and make me truly in earnest. Teach me to keep my eyes fixed on the goal, that no earthly pleasure or gain may shut it out from my sight. Show me what I ought to do, and give me grace to do it. Save me from lazy carelessness and indifference. Teach me to put my heart into my work, and to do it all to Thy glory. Help me to master myself, to conquer my faults, to be a help and blessing to others, that so 'running, not as uncertainly,' I may at last obtain the prize, and be numbered among Thy faithful ones, who having overcome, shall receive the crown of life, for Thy merit's sake. Amen.

Hymn.

Another day begun ;
Lord, grant us grace that we,
Before the setting of the sun,
Redeem the time for Thee.

Another day of toil,
To Thee we owe our powers ;
Keep Thou our souls from guilty soil
Through all the passing hours.

Another day of fear,
For watchful is our foe ;
And sin is strong, and death is near,
And short our time below.

Another day of hope,
For Thou art with us still ;
And Thine Almighty strength can cope
With all who seek our ill.

Another day of grace
To help us on our way,
One step towards the resting-place,
The eternal sabbath-day.

III

Saturday.

HEAVEN OUR HOME.

Text: Ps. xvi. 11.

'In thy presence is fulness of joy, and at thy right hand there are pleasures for evermore.'

Do you think much about your home in heaven? Do you look forward to it? If a man truly believes in it, there is no such splendid comfort, through all the rough toil and struggle of this life.

Down here the best of us fail, and get into trouble. We don't do half we meant; we leave off with our work half finished, our victories half won, and with far more of the mire of sin about us, than we hoped when we started on our road. We get downhearted and tired out, and if it were not for that Home beyond which awaits us, we should often be tempted to leave off trying altogether.

But heaven—how different it will be from all this! Here we have seen the beauty and happiness of goodness faintly, and tried, poorly enough, to reach out after it. There we shall know no failure, no remorse, no weakness. We shall have what here we longed for, and be what here we strove after. The scars, the dust, the wounds, the weariness of this life, will be for ever forgotten in the light of God's countenance. 'Thou shalt give them drink of Thy pleasures as out of a river.'

In this life we are being educated for heaven. That is why God our Father put us here, that we might learn by trial how to bear and how to overcome. Christ Jesus says to each of us, 'I go to prepare a place for you;' and He bids us while we are waiting, to prepare ourselves also for the Home of Peace.

If you truly believe in heaven, you will spend your days here in preparing for it. How can you do that? Simply by putting out of your life everything which makes you unfit for heaven.

In those golden courts, no oath, no impure word may be heard. Give them up then here. In that home no quarrelling, no anger, no selfish brutality, will ever ruffle the peace of the saints. Let them not be known where you are now. If you would be with the white-robed company hereafter, remember that you are called to be a saint now, and let your body be the temple of the Holy Ghost on earth.

For if you never think or care about heaven during your working days, what happiness would it bring you if God were to take you there when you died? Everything which made life pleasant to you here you would have to give up. Everything which bored and wearied you here, would be the endless occupation of the saints.

Here you never prayed, never thanked God, never thought of Him. You loved loafing about and making others work for you. Your favourite haunt was the public-house, where you would spend hours over a pipe and glass of beer. Your favourite companions were wild, riotous young fellows, who liked a drunken frolic, and thought no shame of poaching, of dog-fights, of low music-halls, of worse places still. Heaven would be a place of torment to you, and God will never take you there as you are.

Oh, my friends, you have been reading what Christian manliness is. You have seen what a happy, blessed life it opens out to man here, and what a joyful future in the world to come. For God's sake, be warned in time, and do not spoil and wreck your life for both worlds. Make up your minds at all costs to put God first, and to trample down sin, that so through the love of Jesus Christ you may taste at last in His presence 'the fulness of joy,' and know at His right hand those pleasures which are for evermore.

Prayer.

O God, our Father, who hast prepared for Thy children a home of peace and joy beyond all that heart can hope or wish for, help me so to live down here that I may be worthy to enter into it.

Thou hast called me to be Thy child; purify me even as Thou art pure, that I may not disgrace my Father and my home. Teach me how to live a noble, manly, steadfast life, trampling down sin and laziness, and keeping my eyes fixed on Thee, that so I may do Thy will perfectly, and be ready when Thou shalt call me.

Let the thought of the joys of heaven comfort me in trouble, nerve me in trial, and strengthen me in temptation. Set my heart on attaining them, that I may not squander my eternal happiness for the sake of any earthly gain. Help me to go on from strength to strength, growing in grace, in faith, in love, that so an entrance may be ministered unto me abundantly into the everlasting kingdom of our Lord and Saviour

Heaven our Home.

Jesus Christ, to whom be all glory for evermore. Amen.

HYMN.

Jerusalem, my happy home,
  When shall I come to Thee?
When shall my sorrows have an end,
  Thy joys when shall I see?

Oh, happy harbour of the saints,
  Oh, sweet and pleasant soil;
In thee no sorrow may be found—
  No grief, no care, no toil.

There lust and lucre cannot dwell,
  There envy bears no sway;
There is no hunger, heat, or cold,
  But pleasure every day.

Thy saints with glory shall be crowned—
  Shall see God face to face;
Thy triumph still, they still rejoice,
  Most happy is their case.

Our sweet is mixed with bitter gall,
  Our pleasure is but pain,
Our joys scarce last the looking on,
  Our sorrows still remain.

Thy walls are made of precious stones,
  Thy bulwarks diamond square,
Thy gates are of right orient pearl
  Exceeding rich and rare.

Fourth Week—Saturday.

Thy turrets and thy pinnacles
  With carbuncles do shine;
Thy very streets are paved with gold
  Surpassing clear and fine.

Thy gardens and thy gallant walks
  Continually are green;
There grow such sweet and pleasant flowers
  As nowhere else are seen.

Quite through the streets, with silver sound,
  The flood of life doth flow;
Upon whose banks on every side
  The wood of life doth grow.

There trees for evermore bear fruit,
  And evermore do spring;
There evermore the angels sit,
  And evermore do sing.

Ah, my sweet home, Jerusalem,
  Would God I were in thee!
Would God my woes were at an end,
  And I thy joys might see.

BY THE SAME AUTHOR.

Wives and Mothers;
Or, READINGS FOR MOTHERS' MEETINGS.
FIRST SERIES. Square fcap. 8vo. cloth, 3s. 6d.
SECOND SERIES. Square fcap. 8vo. cloth, 3s. 6d.

'Very practical. Divided into a wife's duties, trials, temptations, and helps, with some cheerful words of good advice on each.'—*Guardian.*

By LADY BAKER (Amy Marryat).

Friendly Words for Our Girls.
7th Thousand. Square fcap. 8vo. limp cloth, 1s. 6d.; paper, 1s.

'Is adapted, and it seems to us with great fitness, to the spiritual wants of young girls of the humbler class—milliners, factory-girls, domestic servants, and so on. Prayers to use on suitable occasions, hymns to read over, and brief paragraphs of wise and kind advice, it provides for this particular class; thoroughly practical.'—*Literary Churchman.*

Lays for the Little Ones.
48mo. cloth, 1s.; sewed, 6d.

'These sweet little poems are admirably adapted for young children, and will, we think, lose nothing by a comparison with Taylor's "Hymns for Infant Minds."'—*Mothers' Treasury.*

By the REV. C. H. RAMSDEN,
Rector of Chilham, Canterbury.

A Manual for Christian Schoolboys.
Containing Short Counsels and Prayers for Private Use.
6th Edit. enlgd. 32mo. 1s.; roan, 2s.; mor. 3s. *Cheap Edition*, 6d.

'An admirable little companion for intelligent and thoughtful lads. The advice given is excellent throughout, and it is so expressed as to attract attention.'—*Review.*

HATCHARDS, PUBLISHERS, 187 PICCADILLY, LONDON.

By M. E. TOWNSEND.

Dedicated to our Working Men, Women, and Children.

Heart and Home Songs. Original and Selected.
BIJOU EDITION, Fcap. 8vo. cloth gilt, 3s. 6d. ; leather, 6s. 6d. to 21s.
CHEAP EDITION FOR WORKING PEOPLE. Fcap. 8vo. limp, 1s. 6d.

LIST OF SUBJECTS AND NUMBER OF POEMS IN EACH :

Songs of Love and Home, 53 — Songs for the Children, 23 — Sacred Songs, 26 — Working Songs, 56 — Songs of Town and Country, 10 — Flower Songs, 23 — Sea and Boat Songs, 16 — Emigrant Songs, 7 — Songs of War, 8 — National Songs, 14 — Ballads, Heroic and Domestic, 18.

EXTRACTS FROM REVIEWS.

'A capital book. . . . Thoroughly wholesome.'—*Church Bells.*
'A selection, copious yet choice, containing poems, old and new, of a simple and practical kind for reading at home.'—*Guardian.*
'An excellent selection.'—*John Bull.*
'One of the nicest collections of songs.'—*Bazaar.*
'An admirable book for use at Penny Readings.'—*Homilist.*
'A book of the right kind. Will bring brightness to many an English home.'
Fireside.
'Welcome especially to the sons and daughters of toil.'—*Hand and Heart.*

*** *Music for above in course of preparation.*

By BISHOP OXENDEN.

1. **Prayers for Private Use.**
   98th Thousand. 32mo. cloth, 1s. ; roan, 2s. ; morocco, 3s.

2. **Fervent Prayer.**
   39th Thousand. 18mo. *large type*, cloth, 1s.

3. **Great Truths in very Plain Language.**
   31st Thousand. 18mo. *large type*, cloth, 1s.

4. **Decision.** 25th Thousand. 18mo. cloth, 1s. 6d.

5. **The Christian Life.**
   42nd Thous. Fcap. 8vo. *large type*, cl. 2s. 6d. ; roan, 5s. ; mor. 7s.
   Cheap Edition, small type, limp, 1s. ; roan, 2s. 6d. ; mor. 4s. 6d.

6. **The Pathway of Safety;**
   Or, COUNSEL TO THE AWAKENED.
   263rd Thous. Fcap. 8vo. *large type*, cl. 2s. 6d. ; roan, 5s. ; mor. 7s.
   Cheap Edition, small type, limp, 1s. ; roan, 2s. 6d. ; mor. 4s. 6d.

HATCHARDS, PUBLISHERS, 187 PICCADILLY, LONDON.

Readings for Mothers' Meetings, &c.

1. **Mothers of Scripture.**
   By Mrs. GOODWIN HATCHARD, Author of 'Prayers for Children,' 'Eight Years' Experience of Mothers' Meetings' (*out of print*), &c. Square fcap. 8vo. 2s. 6d,
   Also the Introduction to above, separately as a Pamphlet, 6d.
   'Mothers' Meetings, and How to Organize them.'
   'Ought to be in the hands of every lady who conducts them.'
   Christian Observer.

2. **Short Words for Long Evenings.**
   By E. WORDSWORTH.
   Large-type Edition. Square fcap. 8vo. cloth extra, 2s. 6d.
   Cheap Edition. 5th Thous. 18mo. small type, cl. extra, 1s. 6d.
   'A remarkable book simply expressed.'—*Guardian.*

3. **Thoughts for the Chimney-corner.**
   By E. WORDSWORTH. (*Large-type Edition out of print.*)
   Cheap Edition. 7th Thous. 18mo. sm. type, cloth extra, 1s. 6d.
   'One of the most delightful books we have come across.'—*John Bull.*

4. **Plain and Pleasant Words.**
   By Author of 'Old Peter Pious,' &c. Sq. fcap. 8vo. cloth, 2s. 6d.
   'Wise and good words; and are well calculated to be useful.'
   Mothers' Treasury.

5. **Fifty-two Addresses for Mothers' Meetings.**
   By Mrs. C. STUART PERRY. Preface by BISHOP PERRY.
   18mo. cloth, 1s. 6d.
   'Useful, not for reading aloud, but for studying before giving an address.'
   Guardian.

6. **Homespun Stories.**
   By CHERITH, Author of 'The Storm-Prayer Appeal,' &c.
   Second Edition. 18mo. cloth, 1s. 6d.
   'Very useful for the parish library.'—*Christian Observer.*
   'Admirable reading.'—*Friendly Leaves.*

7. **Bric-à-Brac Stories.**
   By CHERITH, Author of 'Homespun Stories,' &c. 18mo. cl. 1s. 6d.
   'Interesting and well written.'—*Mothers' Treasury.*

8. **The Christian Mother;**
   Or, NOTES FOR MOTHERS' MEETINGS.
   By the late Mrs. E. HOARE, of Tunbridge Wells.
   Second Edition. 16mo. cloth, 1s.
   'This choice little book—decidedly the best of its kind.'—*Record.*

9. **Prayers for Mothers' Meetings.**
   By Mrs. GOODWIN HATCHARD. Just published. 16mo. 1s.

HATCHARDS, PUBLISHERS, 187 PICCADILLY, LONDON.

3s. 6d. Historical Series for Boys and Girls.

1. Royal Captives.
By CRONA TEMPLE. With Frontispiece.
1. Caractacus. 2. Robert of Normandy. 3. Juana, Queen of Spain. 4. The Last of the Incas. 5. The Lady Elizabeth.

Also in 5 Separate Parts, limp cloth, 1s. each.

'One of the best boys' and girls' books we ever read.'—*Graphic*.

2. Fleur-de-Lis;
Or, Leaves from French History. By ESTHER CARR. Frontispiece.
1. The White Flag in Italy.
2. Catherine de Bourbon.
3. The Minority of Louis XIII.
4. Philippe d'Anjou.

'It would be difficult to find a book more suitable to boys and girls who are fond of history.'—*Standard*.

3. Blameless Knights;
Or, LUTZEN AND LA VENDÉE.
By VISCOUNTESS ENFIELD. Frontispiece.

'Highly interesting historical tales.'—*Court Journal*.

4. Eighty Years Ago.
By H. CAVE, Author of 'Friend-in-Need Papers,' &c.

'An interesting tale of the time of the first French Revolution.'—*Record*.

5. Tales of the Great and Brave.
By MARGARET FRASER-TYTLER. With Frontispiece.

Containing Biographies of Wallace, Bruce, Edward the Black Prince, Joan of Arc, Richard Cœur de Lion, Prince Charles Stuart, Buonaparte, Sobieski, King of Poland, Peter the Great, Washington, Henry de Larochejaquelin, Hofer, and Wellington.

6. The Wooden Walls of Old England;
Or, LIVES OF CELEBRATED ADMIRALS.
By MARGARET FRASER-TYTLER.

Cheap Edition, sq. fcap. 8vo., with Frontispiece, cloth, 2s. 6d.

The Earl's Path.
An Historical Romance for the Young. By SYDNEY CORNER.

'A highly interesting narrative. . . . The love-story, interwoven with the historical facts, is very charming.'—*Public Opinion*.

HATCHARDS, PUBLISHERS, 187 PICCADILLY, LONDON.